SLUGGER SAL'S SLUMP

Story and pictures by

SYD HOFF

Windmill Books and E. P. Dutton
New York

Text and illustrations copyright © 1979 by Syd Hoff
All rights reserved
Published by Windmill Books & E. P. Dutton
2 Park Avenue, New York, New York 10016

Library of Congress Cataloging in Publication Data
Hoff, Sydney
  Slugger Sal's slump.
  SUMMARY: As Slugger Sal slips deeper into a slump,
he wonders if he is washed up as a baseball player.
  [1. Baseball—Fiction] I. Title.
PZ7.H672Sn   [E]   78-26338
ISBN: 0-525-61590-3

Published simultaneously in Canada
by Clarke, Irwin & Company, Limited,
Toronto and Vancouver
Designed by Robert Winsor
Printed in the U.S.A.
10 9 8 7 6 5 4 3 2 1

108779

SLUGGER SAL'S SLUMP

Lately, there was something
wrong with Slugger Sal.
Every time he swung at a ball,
he missed.

KER-PLUNK! went the ball as it
landed in the catcher's mitt.

"Strike three, you're out!" he heard
an umpire say, for the twenty-ninth
time in a row.

For the twenty-ninth time in a row,
Slugger Sal walked back to the
bench with a heavy heart.

"Am I all washed up as a baseball
player?" he wondered.

A cat, the team's mascot, seemed
to be wondering the same thing.

"You're in a slump, but don't let it
worry you," said Mr. Sugarman,
the coach. "You're sure to connect
with the ball next time."

But the next time and the next that
Slugger Sal got up at bat, he only
connected with *air*.

Instead of walking back to the
bench, he wished he could go
walking off a cliff.

"Come on, show some winning
   spirit," said Margaret Ann, the
   third baseman, as the team ran out
   on the field to take their positions.

Slugger Sal stayed behind to talk
to Mr. Sugarman. "Sir, shouldn't
you keep me on the bench?"
he asked.

"No, we need you in the field.
You're the best shortstop we
have," said the coach.

So, Slugger Sal went out on the
field to take his position, too.

But he was so busy thinking about
his slump, he didn't see a ground
ball go past him on his right.

He didn't see another grounder go
past him on his left, either.

"Hey, don't you care if we win or lose?" Margaret Ann hollered over to him.

A pop fly was hit straight up in
the air. It drifted over toward
Slugger Sal.

He just stood there, without
looking up.

"Catch the ball!" shouted the fans.

"Catch the ball!" shouted Mr.
Sugarman, and even the cat
seemed to be shouting.

Margaret Ann had to run over and
catch the ball before it landed on
Slugger Sal's head.

"Maybe I should have let it knock
some sense into you," she said.

The game ended and Slugger Sal's
team walked off the field as if they
were going to a funeral. "Cheer
up, we'll do better tomorrow,"
said Mr. Sugarman.

"Oh, what a slump I'm in. Oh, what a slump I'm in," said Slugger Sal.

Now Mr. Sugarman didn't look so
cheery, himself.

Slugger Sal walked into his house.
"Well, how did your team do
today?" asked his mother and
father.

"All I know is I struck out six more
times," he said. "I'm in a slump.
I'll never be able to hit a ball again."

"Nonsense, your slump will end
sooner or later. No slump lasts
forever," said his mother.

"That's right. The trick is to keep
on trying your best," said his
father, "and never do anything to
hurt your team."

Slugger Sal thought of how he had
been the strong man of his team.

Then he thought of how he had let
them down.

He kept thinking of it while he
took his shower and for hours
afterward.

The next day, the smile on
Slugger Sal's face showed he had
been thinking.

"Come on, team, let's win today,"
he said, before Mr. Sugarman
could say it.

There was no change. Slugger Sal
still struck out a few more times
at bat.

But that didn't stop him from
making some great plays in the
field, and keeping on saying,
"Come on, team, let's win today!"

Then Slugger Sal stepped up to
the plate in the bottom half of the
ninth inning, with the score tied.

CRACK! He connected with the
ball at last!

Slugger Sal ran to first base, then
to second…

The ball was rolling to the fence.
Outfielders were chasing it.

Slugger Sal rounded third. The
ball was on its way to the plate.
"Slide!" cried Mr. Sugarman.

He slid in before the catcher could
tag him. "Safe!" shouted the
umpire.

"I hope you'll always play like that,
even when you're in a slump,"
said Margaret Ann.

"I will," said Slugger Sal, while
the cat licked his face.